The Greatest

by

Alan Gibbons

Illustrated by Dylan Gibson

To Anthony Walker

First published in 2006 in Great Britain by
Barrington Stoke Ltd
18 Walker Street, Edinburgh, EH3 7LP

www.barringtonstoke.co.uk

Reprinted 2008

ISBN: 978-1-84299-390-3

Printed in Great Britain by Bell & Bain Ltd

Contents

Chapter 1
Enemy No.1

My name is Ali.

My hero's name is Ali. He is Muhammad Ali. He's the greatest boxer who ever lived. His poster's on my bedroom wall.

I'm twelve years old. I live in England.

Muhammad Ali was born on January 17th, 1942 in Louisville, Kentucky.

That's in the USA.

I'm a Muslim. So is Muhammad Ali.

Some people blame Muslims for all kinds of things. It was the same for Muhammad Ali. I've had to learn to fight, just like him.

I'm fighting tonight against St John's Club. They're the best club around here. I'm fighting their best boxer. That makes him

the best boxer in this area. There will be three rounds. I feel sick. Yes, I'm sick with nerves.

Muhammad Ali started boxing when he was twelve. Somebody stole his new bike so he went looking for a policeman. The cop was called Joe Martin. When Muhammad Ali found him, Martin was teaching boys to box. Muhammad Ali liked what he saw and joined in. One day he would be the greatest World Heavyweight Champion ever.

Someone stole my bike too, and I know who did it. It was a lad called Chris Keane. He stole it when I was riding it. He was with his gang. They pushed me off my bike and took it. The next week, I started boxing so no one would ever take anything from me again. Tonight I fight Keane. One of us will be the area champion. I hope it's me.

Keane hates Muslim kids. He hates
anyone he thinks is different. He picks on
kids with red hair or glasses. Most of all, he
picks on kids like me. He calls me a Paki. He
says I'm a terrorist. He says I'm like Osama
Bin Laden. But I'm no terrorist. I'm twelve!
I'm just a normal kid. I like football,
computer games and boxing. I just want to
be left alone. I want to be a man of peace. I
want to be like Muhammad Ali.

I start packing my stuff. See my hands are shaking. I look up at my poster of Muhammad Ali. Did your hands shake, champ? How did you feel before a fight? I wish you could tell me.

"Are you ready, Ali?" Dad calls.

"Yes, I'm coming," I tell him.

I look at the poster of Muhammad Ali again. *Wish me luck, champ.*

I jog down the stairs and follow Dad to the car. It's a taxi. That's what Dad does for a living. He drives taxis round town. He's been called a Paki too. He doesn't fight. He says it's best to ignore the men who say it. He doesn't like trouble. Neither do I. But I'm not going to walk away. I'm not going to let people take what's mine.

Dad starts the car. I watch the town flash by. That's the street where Keane took my bike off me. I got it back in the end. Dad sorted it out for me. He went round Keane's house and spoke to his dad. But the frame was bent. Keane did that on purpose. He wanted to upset me.

He did that all right. I felt ashamed. Dad shouldn't have to stand up for me. I should be able to do that for myself. I swore I would learn to stick up for myself. Tonight I will.

"Are you nervous?" Dad asks.

"Me? No," I say.

He knows I'm not telling the truth. My voice goes funny when I'm going to fight. It's OK once I'm in the ring. It's the bit before the fight, the build-up that gets to me. My hands go clammy. The back of my neck gets hot. Even my legs shake a bit. I feel as if I'm falling to bits. But I don't.

When I'm in the ring I'm cool. I hit fast and dance away. I've won all my fights this year. I'm like my hero Muhammad Ali, a winner. I remember what he said:

Float like a butterfly,
Sting like a bee.

When Keane comes out of his corner, I'm going to float. When he gets tired, I'm going to sting. He won't hurt me. I won't let him.

At last, we're at St John's Hall. This is Chris Keane's home ground. He took my bike from me that time. He thinks he's hard. He thinks he can do anything to me. He thinks he's going to win.

But he's in for a surprise.

Muhammad Ali – the early years

Muhammad Ali was born Cassius Marcellus Clay on January 17th, 1942 in Louisville, Kentucky.

At that time black people in many parts of the USA were seen as second-class citizens. They had to use different seats on the bus and in restaurants. They did not have the same right to vote as white people.

In 1954, when Muhammad Ali was twelve, his bike was stolen.

He went to the police.

Officer Joe Martin said he would teach him to box.

By the time Ali was eighteen years old, he had won two National Golden Gloves crowns and two National AAU titles.

In **1960**, when he was eighteen, Ali won an **Olympic Gold Medal**.

Chapter 2
Nerves

When I walk into the changing rooms
Jerry Feeney comes over. He's our coach. He
was a boxer himself. You only have to look
at his nose. One day he asked me why I
wanted to box. I said I hated Keane. Jerry
said hate is for losers. You have to love
yourself. He showed me how to get fit. I did
press-ups and tuck jumps. I did pike jumps
and star jumps. I did lots of stuff like that.

He taught me to move. He taught me not to lose my temper. He taught me discipline.

"How are you going, Ali?" he says.

Jerry doesn't care if you're a Muslim. He just wants you to be a good kid. That's what he always tells me and the other boys.

"Just be a good kid. Stay out of trouble."

I want to tell him I'm fine. But he'll know I'm lying.

"I'm nervous," I tell him. "I've got butterflies."

"Good," Jerry says. "You can use that. It will give you an edge. If you get too cool or too cocky, you lose. Look what happened to Muhammad Ali against Ken Norton."

I've seen the DVD. Dad bought them all for me, every fight Ali ever had. Norton

beat Ali when Ali was getting old. Ali didn't train hard enough. He got lazy but he got punished for it. In that fight, Norton broke his jaw.

"Yes," I say, "Norton beat Ali but Ali got his revenge."

Norton beat Ali in March 1973. A few months later, Ali was back. He beat Norton in October the same year. Keane took my bike last year. This year I'll beat him. I don't hate him any more but I won't let him push me around.

"Anyway," Jerry says, "get changed, son." Dad takes the hint. He's the boss until I get to the gym. Then Jerry takes over. He's my boxing dad.

I can hear people coming into the hall. There will be five or six fights. All the boys' dads will be there. Then there are the coaches and some others. That's a lot of people watching. Now I'm more nervous than ever. My shirt sticks to my back. It's the sweat.

That's when Keane walks in. He's got his hair all spiked up, full of gel. He's done it just for our fight. He looks at me and grins. It isn't a nice smile. Then he carries on round the corner. He thinks I'm scared of him. He thinks I'm beaten already. I'm going to prove him wrong.

Some of the other boys try to talk to me.
I don't want to know. I just want to shut my
eyes and see the ring. There will be Keane
and me facing one another. He'll come after
me. Hunter and hunted. Predator and prey.
I'll have to dance. I'll have to bob and
weave. He's strong so I have to stay away
early on. I have to take the sting out of his
punches.

"Make him work," Jerry says. "You're not going to fight. You're going to box."

I nod. He's told me that before.

There are three fights before mine. I watch the boys go out to fight. I watch them come back. They're excited if they win. They look let down if they lose. One boy looks as if he's crying. He sees me watching and turns red. I won't cry. I won't lose, that's why.

Hey, that sounds like one of Ali's poems:

I won't cry.
I won't lose –
That's why!

I go to pee. For ages it won't come. That's another sign of nerves. A member of our club comes in and looks in the mirror. His cheek is swollen and red.

"Did you win?" I ask.

"No," he says. "I lost. He was too strong for me. Keep an eye on Chris Keane, Ali. He's the best they've got."

I know that already. His dad was a boxer. So were his brothers. It runs in the family. All his family will be in the hall, cheering him on. I've only got Dad. Mum doesn't come. It wouldn't be right.

I wait until I'm on my own. I look in the mirror. How will *my* face look after the fight?

"Ali?" Jerry calls. "Anybody seen Ali?"

"I'm here," I say.

"Come and get your gloves on," Jerry says. "You're up next."

I nod. He's holding my bright red boxing gloves. When I hold out my hands they shake a bit. He pretends not to see.

"This boy you're going to fight is a bully," Jerry says. "He's a bit like Sonny Liston was in the old days."

Sonny Liston is the guy Muhammad Ali beat to become World Heavyweight Champion. They say Sonny Liston hung around with gangsters. Everyone was scared of him. Not Ali. He beat Liston twice. He knocked him out both times.

"Bullies get beaten," Jerry says. "You've just got to use your loaf."

My loaf. That's what Jerry calls my head. He means I've got to box clever. No problem.

Muhammad Ali's
road to the championship

October 29th, 1960 Ali beat Tunny Hunsacker.

December 27th, 1960 Ali beat Herb Sile.

January 17th, 1961 Ali beat Tony Esperti.

February 7th, 1961 Ali beat Jim Robinson.

February 21st, 1961 Ali beat Donnie Freeman.

April 19th, 1961 Ali beat Lamar Clark.

June 26th, 1961 Ali beat Duke Sabedong.

July 22nd, 1961 Ali beat Alonzo Johnson.

October 7th, 1961 Ali beat Alex Miteff.

November 29th, 1961 Ali beat Willi Besmanoff.

February 10th, 1962 Ali beat Sonny Banks.

February 28th, 1962 Ali beat Don Warner.

April 23rd, 1962 Ali beat George Logan.

May 19th, 1962 Ali beat Billy Daniels.

July 29th, 1962 Ali beat Alejandro Lavorante.

November 15th, 1962 Ali beat Archie Moore.

January 24th, 1963 Ali beat Charlie Powell.

March 13th, 1963 Ali beat Doug Jones.

June 18th, 1963 Ali beat Henry Cooper.

February 25th, 1964 Ali beat Sonny Liston to become Heavyweight Champion of the World.

ALI $\overline{\text{VRS}}$ LISTON

WORLD'S HEAVYWEIGHT CHAMPIONSHIP BOUT!!!
SEE THE BIG PUNCHES
FEB 25TH

Chapter 3
Face Off

When Muhammad Ali fought Sonny Liston they thought he had no chance. Liston was mean and tough. He was unbeatable. Bets were seven to one against Ali. Ali didn't care. He called Liston a big, ugly bear. Ali wore a robe that said "Bear Hunting". Keane is a big, ugly bear too. I'm going bear hunting.

"Are you ready?" Jerry asks.

"I'm ready."

I follow him to the ring. I see Keane's
dad and his brothers. They're smiling. They
shake their heads. They're saying I've got
no chance. I'm going to show them. I duck
through the ropes and climb into the ring.
When I lift my head Keane is looking right
at me. His eyes are hard. I see his lips move.
I know what he's saying.

Paki.

I'm going to stop him doing that. I don't hate him. So why does he have to hate me? Why does he have to call me names? I've never done him any harm. I just want to be left alone.

I go to the middle of the ring. The ref explains a few things. We touch gloves and go back to our corners. In three rounds one of us is going to be area champ. I want it to be me. I want that so much. I want Keane to know I'm as good as him, maybe even better.

When the bell goes Keane comes out first. He rushes across the ring and starts throwing punches. They're wild and most of the time they miss. Lots of kids give up the moment Keane comes at them. He scares them silly. I'm different. I'm using my loaf. I dance away, just like Ali. I see Jerry nodding. *Don't fight, box.* Keane comes after me. I jab at him, a left then a right. The punches don't stop him. He keeps coming. I keep dancing. I move round the ring, keeping out of the corners. I don't want him to trap me where he can land a punch.

One time I catch a word.

"Coward," he mouths.

I meet his look.

It means stand and fight. I glance at
Jerry. I know what he wants. *Don't fight.
Box.* That's what I'm going to do. I'm going
to stay away from Keane. I'm going to
move. I'm going to outbox him.

Trouble is, Keane doesn't know that. He
just keeps coming at me, like a big, ugly
bear. He follows me the way Joe Frazier
followed Ali. Smokin' Joe Frazier was the
first man to beat Ali. That time, Ali wasn't

just fighting Frazier. He was fighting the American Government too.

Ali had defended his title ten times. No one could beat him. Then the Government wanted him to join the army. Ali refused. He said he was a Muslim. He wanted peace. America was fighting a war against a small country called Vietnam. Ali refused to go. So they took his title away. For over three years he wasn't allowed to box. He lost the best years of his sporting life.

When he was allowed to box again, he fought Joe Frazier. Joe was tough and hard to hurt. He followed Ali around the ring and knocked him down once. Ali got up. He went on boxing. After fifteen rounds Ali lost on points. Some people call it the greatest fight of all time.

I watch Keane following me round. He'd like to knock me down. He'd like to see me flat on my back. It isn't going to happen.

The bell goes. As we pass each other, Keane whispers: "Stand and fight, Osama."

I don't say anything. But I hate the way he calls me that.

Ali loses his title

After that first fight with Liston, Ali became a Muslim. He changed his name from Cassius Clay to Muhammad Ali. A lot of the newspapers hated him for that.

On May 25th, 1965, there was a rematch with Sonny Liston. Ali beat him by a knock out in round one.

November 22nd, 1965 Ali beat Floyd Patterson.

March 29th, 1966 he beat George Chuvalo.

May 21st, 1966 he beat Henry Cooper.

August 6th, 1966 he beat Brian London.

September 10th, 1966 he beat Karl Mildenberger.

November 12th, 1966 he beat Cleveland Williams.

February 6th, 1967 he beat Ernie Terrell.

March 22nd, 1967 he beat Zora Folley.

Then, from 1967 to 1970, Ali was banned from boxing. He had refused to join the US Army.

He said, "Why should they ask me to put on a uniform and go ten thousand miles from home and drop bombs and bullets on brown people in Vietnam while so-called Negro people in Louisville are treated like dogs?"

In 1970 the American courts changed their mind. Muhammad Ali was allowed to box again.

October 26th, 1970 he beat Jerry Quarry.

December 7th, 1970 he beat Oscar
Bonavena.

March 8th, 1971 he lost to Joe
Frazier over fifteen rounds. It was his
first defeat as a professional.

Chapter 4
Fists of Fury

At the end of the first round I go back to the corner and sit on my stool.

"You're doing well," Jerry says.

"He wants me to stand and fight," I say. "He's started calling me names."

"I'll talk to the ref," Jerry says. "That's not allowed."

"No," I tell him. "Don't. I don't want any help. I can beat him my way."

Jerry nods.

"It's up to you, son."

He leans over.

"But don't lose your temper," he says. "That's what the boy wants. He's clumsy. If you stand and swap punches, he'll win. But if you dance, you win. He's stronger but you're faster."

Jerry squeezes my hand.

"There's something else," he says. "I've noticed something."

"What?" I ask.

"When Keane throws his right hand," Jerry says, "he drops the left."

"So?" I ask.

"Simple," Jerry explains. "If you throw a right-hand punch, he's got no defence. You'll get him."

I tell him I'll remember. But when I get to the middle of the ring Keane's doing it again. He mouths an insult. The ref doesn't see. I stop moving and swing at him. The punch doesn't hurt him. But when he hits me back, it hurts like mad. I've been stupid. I'm not boxing. I'm fighting. He hits me in the ribs and I feel my legs wobble.

Jerry's saying something to me. *Dance.*
Yes, dance like Ali. I move away. It isn't
easy. My legs feel weak. But I get away from
him. My neck's hot. I feel stupid. I fell for it.
Keane made me fight.

But it isn't over. Ali lost to Joe Frazier.
But he came back. He beat Frazier twice
after that. I'm not finished yet. I'm going to
turn this round.

I dance and Keane follows me. He
catches me once but the punch doesn't land
properly. I swerve and get away.

That's when I hear Keane breathing. He's
puffing and panting. It's the first time he's
looked tired. Hey, I could win this fight. I
skip round him, jabbing. He's slowing down.
He can't come after me the way he did.
After two rounds of swinging punches he's
running out of steam.

Muhammad Ali takes his title back

July 26th, 1971 Ali beat Jimmy Ellis.

November 17th, 1971 Ali beat Buster Mathis.

December 26th, 1971 Ali beat Jurgen Blin.

April 1st, 1972 Ali beat Mac Foster.

May 1st, 1972 Ali beat George Chuvalo.

June 27nd, 1972 Ali beat Jerry Quarry.

July 19th, 1972 Ali beat Al 'Blue' Lewis.

September 20th, 1972 Ali beat Floyd Patterson.

November 21st, 1972 Ali beat Bob Foster.

February 14th, 1973 Ali beat Joe Bugner.

March 31st, 1973 Ali lost to Ken Norton.

September 10th, 1973 Ali beat Ken Norton.

October 20th, 1973 Ali beat Rudi Lubbers.

Jan 28th, 1974 Ali beat Joe Frazier.

These fourteen fights meant Ali could have another go at winning the World Heavyweight Title.

He had to fight a former US Marine, George Foreman.

Every one thought Foreman was unbeatable. He had never lost. He had won with 10 knockouts in the first round, 11 in the second round and 11 in the third or fourth.

He'd also knocked out Joe Frazier and Ken Norton, two men who had beaten Ali.

The fight between Ali and George Foreman was held in Zaire, in Africa. They called it the 'Rumble in the Jungle'.

Ali surprised everyone. He didn't dance this time. He lay on the ropes and took every punch Foreman threw. He called it the 'rope a dope'.

In the eighth round Ali came off the ropes and knocked Foreman out.

He was World Heavyweight Champion for the second time.

Chapter 5
Final Countdown

It's the third and last round. Keane doesn't look happy. Jerry says I'm just ahead on points. My punches don't hurt Keane much but they score points. He keeps missing and I keep scoring. He's tired too. It's all that swinging and missing.

The bell rings for the round to start and we come out of our corners. I see Keane's

dad and his brothers. They're talking about
the fight. This time, they're not smiling.

Keane has to catch me and land some
punches. I try to dance away. Trouble is, I'm
tired too. Keane catches me with a right
hand. I flop against the ropes and he moves
in. He hits me again.

I suck in my breath. Then I see Jerry.

"Dance," he says. "Dance."

I try but Keane puts his arm round mine and swings me back. That's when I remember what Jerry said. When Keane throws his right hand, he drops the left.

He has no defence. I see him throw the right. So I lean back.

Jerry's right. Keane's wide open. I put everything into a right-hand punch to the rib cage.

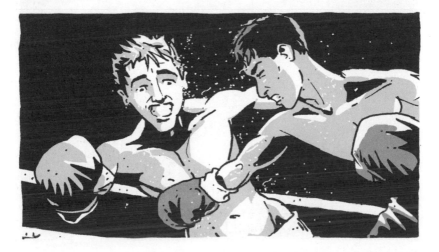

Keane gasps and stops dead. He's not smiling now. That's all I need. I skip away and hit him with a right and a left. They don't hurt but I'm off the ropes. I scored too.

Keane tries to follow me. He's swinging with both hands. Every time he tries to get me, he misses. Jerry's smiling. Keane's dad is shaking his head. Then I see Dad. It's the first time I've noticed him. He nods to me. I'm winning.

I remember something about Ali. A boxer called Ernie Terrell called him his old name, Cassius Clay, not Muhammad Ali. Ali beat him. After every punch Ali kept saying: "What's my name?"

As I skip past Keane I whisper in his ear.

"I'm not Osama," I whisper. "What's my name?"

Then I hit him twice. Left, right. The punches aren't hard but they score.

The bell rings. The ref lifts my arm. I've won.

Muhammad Ali's career ends

March 24th, 1975 Ali beat Chuck Wepner.

May 16th, 1975 Ali beat Ron Lyle.

June 30th, 1975 Ali beat Joe Bugner.

September 30th, 1975 Ali beat Joe Frazier in the 'Thriller in Manila'. Both men said the fight was so hard they felt like they were dying.

February 20th, 1976 Ali beat Jean Coopman.

April 30th, 1976 Ali beat Jimmy Young.

May 24th, 1976 Ali beat Richard Dunn.

September 28th, 1976 Ali beat Ken Norton.

May 16th, 1977 Ali beat Alfredo Evangelista.

September 29th, 1977 Ali beat Earnie Shavers.

February 15th, 1978 Ali lost his title to Leon Spinks. This was a big shock because Spinks was unknown. By then, Ali was 36 years old. People thought he was too old to come back again and become champ.

September 15th, 1978 Ali proved them wrong. He came back the way he had after the Frazier and Norton fights. He beat Leon Spinks and took back his title. He was the first man to win the World Heavyweight Championship three times.

After that, Ali retired but came back and boxed again after eighteen months.

He loved the roar of the crowd too much.

It was a mistake. Boxers are young men. By this time, Ali was too old. He'd had too many hard fights. He lost twice then retired again, for the last time.

October 2nd, 1980 Ali lost to Larry Holmes.

December 11th, 1981 Ali lost to Trevor Berbick. It was his last fight.

Later in life, Ali suffered from Parkinson's disease. Many people think this is because of all the punches he took to the head. All these years later, in spite of his illness, he is still one of the most famous men in the world. He lit the torch at the 1996 Olympics and led the American bid for the 2012 Olympics.

He travels the world and everywhere he goes people want to hear what he has to say.

He is much more than just a sportsman.

Chapter 6
Result

Jerry puts his arm round my shoulder.

"You did well, champ," he says.

I like the way he says it. *Champ.*

Dad comes over too.

"Well done, son," he says. "You didn't lose your temper."

"I did once," I say.

Dad laughs.

"I know, but you got over it," he says.

I leave the ring and get changed. All the other boys come over to shake my hand or slap my back. This must be why Ali kept boxing. I feel like a hero.

We are walking to the car when Chris Keane comes over with his dad. My stomach turns over. I don't want any trouble.

"My son's got something to say to you," Keane's dad says.

Keane doesn't look too happy. His dad nudges him.

"Well done," Keane says. "You were the better boxer."

He grits his teeth. He doesn't like saying it. There's something else. He really hates having to talk to me about it.

"I'm sorry I said those things," Keane says.

His dad takes over.

"My son had no right to insult you," he says. "This is boxing, not gang warfare. It's meant to be a sport. Now shake hands."

I take Keane's hand. He doesn't smile. I don't think he's changed all that much. He'd still be a bully if he could. But there's something in the way.

Me.

I'm the greatest.

Muhammad Ali –
the greatest of all time

Muhammad Ali won 20 world heavyweight title fights.

For the years when he was fighting there were seven different US Presidents.

He fought in a time when there were other great fighters. Men like Sonny Liston, Joe Frazier and George Foreman are legends too.

He's the only man to win three World Heavyweight Championships.

He won his third title when he was 36 years and 8 months old.

He gave up his first title because he thought the war in Vietnam was wrong.

He became a symbol of the fight against racism.

He became a hero to everyone - black and white people, Muslims and non-Muslims.

He wasn't allowed to box for three and a half years, but he still came back to win the world title twice more.

Today he is one of the most loved athletes of all time.

The things Muhammad Ali said

"I'm so great, I impress even
myself."

"I'm young, I'm handsome, I'm
fast. I can't possibly be beat."

"Float like a butterfly,
Sting like a bee,
His hands can't hit
What his eyes can't see."

When asked, during his three and a
half year lay-off, if he missed boxing,

"No, boxing misses me."

After his 'Thriller in Manila' with Joe Frazier,

"It was like death. The closest thing to dying that I know of."

About war,

"How can I kill somebody when I pray five times a day for peace?"

About refusing to join the army,

"I just wanted to be free. And I made a stand all people, not just black people, should have thought about making."

About racism,

"But there's still hatred, and hating someone because of his colour is wrong. It's wrong both ways - it don't matter what colour does the hating. All people, all colours, got to work to get along."

Muhammad Ali to Martin Luther King, the Civil Rights leader,

"In your struggle for freedom, justice and equality, I am with you."

About retiring,

"Father Time caught up with me. I'm finished - we all grow old."

AUTHOR AND ILLUSTRATOR
FACT FILES

VS

ALAN GIBBONS   **DYLAN GIBSON**

ROUND ONE

If you were a boxer, what would your theme tune be?
AG: "Eye of the Tiger".
DG: "Hit Me With Your Rhythm Stick" by Ian Dury and the Blockheads.

ROUND TWO

If you were a boxer, what would your nickname be?
AG: Gladiator.
DG: The Pacifist. I could talk my way out of the fight, not throw a punch!

ROUND THREE

What's your favourite fight from a book or film?

AG: Robert DeNiro fighting in Raging Bull.

DG: The bit in Indiana Jones where he shoots the guy swishing around with his sword.

ROUND FOUR

What would you fight for?

AG: Freedom.

DG: Muhammad Ali used his fame to promote human rights. That's a good thing to fight for!

ROUND FIVE

If you could fight anyone in the world, who would it be? And why?

AG: Anyone from Big Brother.

DG: Captain Kirk from Star Trek – he's a cool guy!

RESULT - *DRAW!!!*

LM 06/09

Barrington Stoke would like to thank all its readers for commenting on the manuscript before publication and in particular:

David Addison
Robbie Bond
Jessica Brennan
James Buckland
Marcus Callow
Joe Castle
Jordan Davies
Emma Fenton
Chloe Hanson
Lucy Harrop
Nick Harrington
Lucy Holmes
Joanne Hover
James Lewis
Jonathon Lewis

Michael Lewis
Conor Makinson
Emma Metcalfe
Thomas Miller
Dominic Murray
Neil Musk
Seb Newman
Phody Papa-Adams
Ashley Parry
Isabelle Sayers
Amy Sharpe
Hazel Stein
Billy Townsend
Lyne Varley
Natalie Weatherhead

Become a Consultant!

Would you like to give us feedback on our titles before they are published? Contact us at the email address below – we'd love to hear from you!

info@barringtonstoke.co.uk
www.barringtonstoke.co.uk